The Magic of Lenka's Wool Socks

Magdalena Georgieva
Gabriela Yancheva

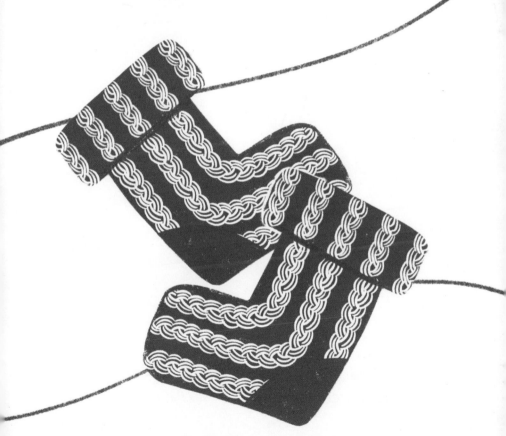

Sofia/Boston
2020

to our grandparents

Meet Lenka.
She lives with her mother
in a small apartment, hidden away
in a quiet neighborhood.

Lenka loves to wear
her mismatched outfits:
some are hand-me-downs
from relatives,
some are gifts from friends,

and a few purchased
in a regular clothing store.

meow?

But most of all, Lenka likes to wear her colorful wool socks, knitted by her grandma Nana.

When she puts them on,
strange things happen.
Cats follow her around.

THIS WAY

She reads long books faster than anyone she's ever met.

THIS WAY

THAT WAY

If she gets lost on the way home, the unknown doesn't scare her.

One day Lenka decided
her socks needed a good scrub.
So she put them in the wash
with the rest of the laundry.

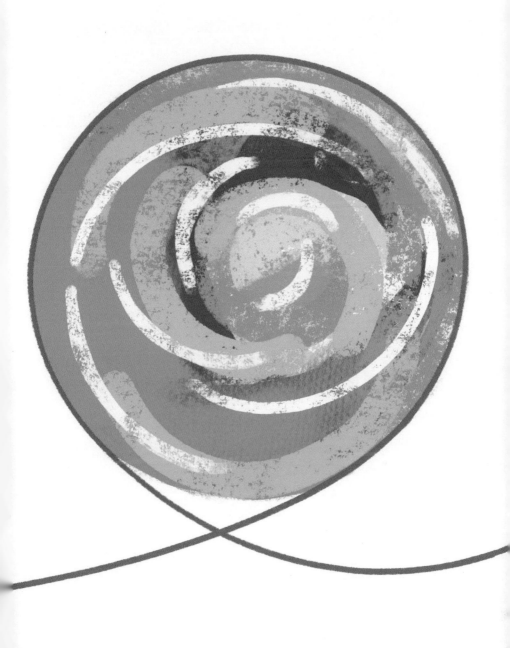

Do you know what happens
to wool in the dryer?

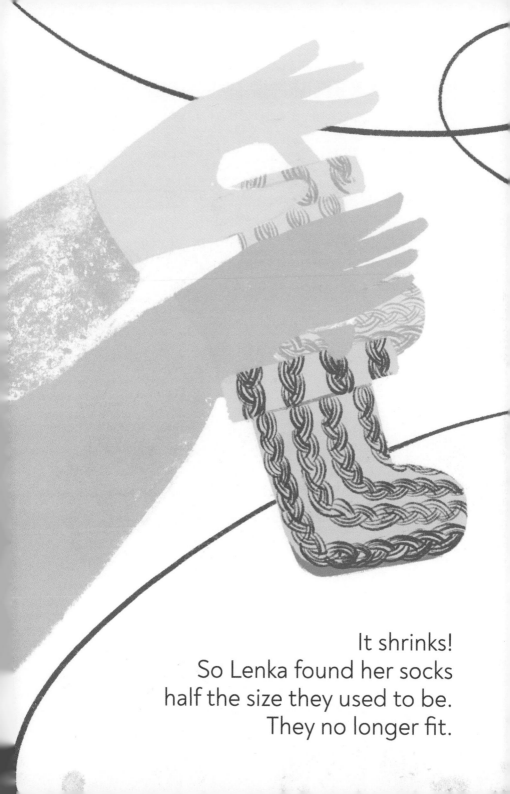

It shrinks!
So Lenka found her socks
half the size they used to be.
They no longer fit.

Everything seemed to have lost
its magic now.

ps-ps..?

Cats no longer followed her around,

books were a bore

and the road home was long and scary.

Lenka grew sad and gloomy,
and Nana noticed.

"Sorry, grandma.
I ruined the wool socks
you knitted me," Lenka confessed.

"Surely that's something we can fix!"
said Nana and got to work.

She grabbed a couple
of red and yellow yarn balls
lying around in her closet and,
stitch after stitch,
she knitted a new pair of socks.

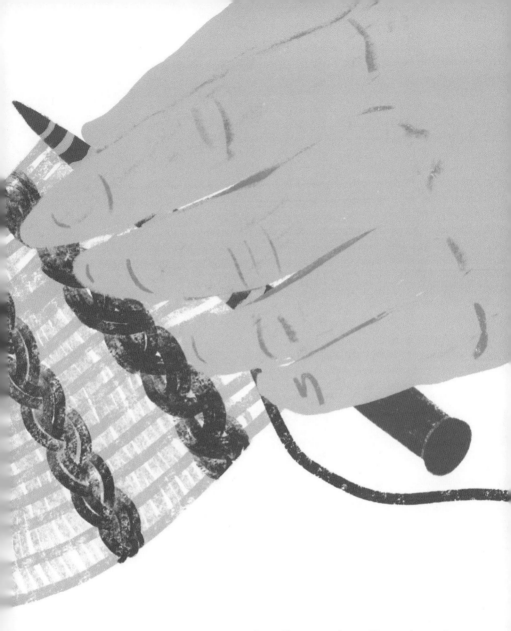

Just before she finished,
she secretly wove a gold string
into the colorful pattern
and whispered,

"May you always be surrounded by friends. May you always be hungry for knowledge. May you never fear getting lost."

Once Lenka put on
her new pair of socks,
everything fell back into place.

Kitties followed her around,

books were sweeter than ever

and she didn't mind being a bit lost at times.

Ever since that day
Lenka learned an important lesson:
never put wool socks
in the dryer!

the End

Printed in Great Britain
by Amazon